Miniature Horses

Miniature Horses

Dorothy Hinshaw Patent
Photographs by William Muñoz

COBBLEHILL BOOKS/DUTTON

New York

For Wanda and Bill Nooney,
who love all animals, especially little ones.

Acknowledgments

The author and photographer want to thank Barbara Ashby and the American Miniature Horse Association for all their help with this book; Laura Van Horn for her photos; Lou Tuckman and the Northwest Miniature Horse Club; Winners' Circle Ranch, especially Barbara Norman; Mel Riley; and NFC Miniature Horse Farm, Brewer Family Miniatures, and The Li'l Horse Ranch (Ron and Sami Scheuring) for use of photos of their horses.

Picture Credits
AMHA, pages 8 (top), 10, 20, 44; Dorothy Hinshaw Patent, 18, 42; and Laura Van Horn, 22, 30. All other photographs are by William Muñoz.

Library of Congress Cataloging-in-Publication Data
Patent, Dorothy Hinshaw.
Miniature horses / Dorothy Hinshaw Patent ; photographs by William Muñoz.
p.   cm.   Includes index.
Summary: Describes the origins and physical characteristics of the
miniature horse, its breeding and care, and its role as work horse,
show horse, and pet.
ISBN 0-525-65049-0
1. Miniature horses—Juvenile literature. [1. Miniature horses. 2. Horses.] I. Muñoz, William, ill. II. Title.
SF293.M56P37 1991 636.1—dc20 90-38641 CIP AC

Published in the United States by
Cobblehill Books, an affiliate of Dutton Children's Books,
a division of Penguin Books USA Inc.

Designer: Jean Krulis
Printed in Hong Kong   First Edition
10 9 8 7 6 5 4 3 2 1

Contents

A miniature horse is the same size as some dogs.

1
Creating a New Breed

Can you imagine a full-grown horse no bigger than a large dog? A baby horse small enough to pick up and carry? Today, there are thousands of such animals in the world, and they're called miniature horses.

Horses and Ponies

Miniature horses are not the same as ponies. A pony is a horse that is shorter than 58 inches at the top of the shoulders. Most ponies look different from riding horses. They have wide, strong bodies. Their necks are usually muscular, and their legs are short for their size. There are many kinds of ponies, some taller than others. The Welsh pony can be 58 inches tall. The American Shetland, on the other hand, isn't taller than 46 inches.

The miniature horse is something different. First of all, it is shorter than the smallest ponies. A mini must be no taller than 34 inches, measured at the top of the shoulders, where the mane ends. A full-grown mini weighs between 150 and 250 pounds. Although some minis resemble ponies, the goal of miniature horse breeders is to create a tiny horse, with everything about it the same as a full-

A miniature horse and a Clydesdale, one of the largest horse breeds.

A mini all fixed up for show.

sized horse, only smaller. They should not have short legs, thick necks, or big bellies.

A Wealth of Color

Miniature horses come in every possible horse color. Many horse breeds allow only certain colors, For example, an Arabian horse, Quarter Horse, or a Thoroughbred cannot have patches of color like a pinto or spots like an Appaloosa. But variety in color is encouraged in minis. They can have Appaloosa spots, pinto patches, solid colors, or they can be beautiful tan buckskins with dark legs, manes, and tails. Some colors that are rare in other breeds are common in minis, such as dark bodies with white or cream manes and tails. In miniature horse shows, there are even special competitions for the most colorful horses.

Kinds of Minis

When miniature horses first became popular in the late 1970s, some looked like riding horses while others resembled draft horses. These two types were both popular, but the most important thing was small size. A horse that was small was valuable, even if its legs were too short or its belly too big. But things have changed since then. Now, a well-proportioned body and a beautiful head are just as important as size, and there are thousands of beautiful minis.

Today, miniature horse breeders are working mainly for two riding-horse types. The first kind looks similar to a sturdy Quarter Horse, called a stock-horse type because Quarter Horses are used to work with livestock like cattle. These animals have muscular legs and broad chests.

SOME OF THE TOP STALLIONS ILLUSTRATE A LITTLE OF THE VARIETY IN MINIATURE HORSE COLORS.

Rowdy, sire of American Miniature Horse Association (AMHA) National Grand Champions, lives at NFC Miniature Horse Farm.

Hemlock Brooks Egyptian King, an AMHA National Grand Champion Stallion, is owned by NFC Miniature Horse Farm.

Orion Light Van'T Huttenest, another famous sire of AMHA National Grand Champions, belongs to Brewer Family Miniatures.

The second type has finer bones and a slimmer body. Its head looks more like that of an Arabian horse, with a delicate muzzle and large eyes. The front of its face is "dished," meaning that it dips in below the forehead. This is called the refined type.

Some minis are muscular, like Quarter Horses.

Others have a lighter build, more like an Arabian.

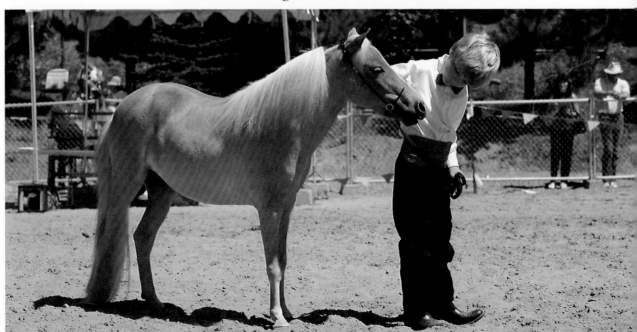

A miniature stallion relaxes at home at Winner's Circle Ranch in Petaluma, CA.

Where Do Minis Come From?

The American Miniature Horse Association, which keeps track of most of the minis in the world, began in 1978. But long before that, many people in different countries were trying to create tiny horses. They used a variety of sources for breeding. Small horses and ponies had been used to work in coal mines in England and Holland. Some of these were brought to the United States in the nineteenth century. They were used in coal mines in the southern states as recently as 1950. The tunnels in mines are small, and full-sized horses were too big to enter them.

Small horses had also been pets of European royalty. Breeders of the American Miniature Horse have imported minis from Holland, West Germany, Belgium, and England for breeding. In Brazil, the Falabella family bred small horses by crossing Thoroughbreds with Shetland ponies. All these varieties—small horses, European minis, ponies, and Falabella horses—went into the breeding of the American Miniature Horse.

After the American Miniature Horse Association was started, breeding of minis became more organized. The association began keeping records of the progress of the breed. Breeders joined the association and sent in information about their horses. When a new foal was born, it had to be "registered" with the association to be called an American Miniature Horse. That meant filling out forms giving the important facts about the foal—who its parents were, when it was born, what color it was. Only horses that stayed small— no more than 34 inches by the time they were five years old—were allowed to be called miniatures.

At first, any horse small enough could be registered as a miniature horse. But as more and more minis looked better and better, things

A mini foal looks just like any other.

changed. The association altered its rules so that now only horses with registered parents can be registered themselves. There is only one exception to this rule. A horse at least five years old that is no taller than 34 inches can be registered if the owners are willing to pay a special fee.

The American Miniature Horse has become a true breed, a special new kind of horse. Minis are popular in many countries in addition to the United States—Canada, England, Holland, Japan, Australia, and several South American countries especially.

Because they are so small, miniature foals appeal to children and adults alike.

2
Real Horses

It may be small, but a miniature is still a real horse. Minis like to be outdoors, in pastures where they can graze. They also can be put in barn stalls, but the stalls are much smaller than those of regular horses. Everything about minis is small except their personality and spirit. Their hooves are dainty, and their soft noses can fit into your hand. A small child can look a miniature horse right in the eyes.

Miniature Foals

Like full-sized mares, female minis usually have their babies, called foals, in the springtime. And just like other horses, minis give birth eleven months after mating. A newborn miniature horse only weighs about 20 pounds and stands between 16 and 21 inches tall. It's easy to pick one up and carry it like a human baby or a puppy. But the little foal is all horse. Soon after birth, it is standing on its own four feet and nuzzling its mother, looking for milk. In a few hours, it can dash around the pasture and buck and jump in the crisp spring air.

The young horse stays with its mother for a few months and plays

Miniature mares waiting to give birth.

Miniature foals are small enough to be easily carried.

with the other foals in the pasture. Its owners hope that it doesn't grow too quickly. A weanling mini—a foal that is old enough to be taken away from its mother and is eating grass and grain instead of milk—can't be called a miniature horse if it is taller than 30 inches at the shoulders. When it is a year old, it can't be more than 32 inches tall.

*A **mini foal** nurses.*

Miniature horse foals are naturally friendly.

Watching Foals Grow

The owners also watch closely to see how the foals grow. Since some of the animals from which the miniature horse began had short legs and big bodies, some minis today have legs that are too short for their bodies or bodies that look too long for the shorter legs. Some also have rounded bellies like Shetland ponies. Animals that look like this are not as valuable as those with the same proportions as a full-sized horse. But they make perfectly good pets for people that are not interested in showing their horses.

One problem that miniature horse owners worry about is the possibility of having dwarf foals. A dwarf is different from a miniature. Its teeth often don't match up properly for good chewing. A dwarf may have a head too big for its neck and a pot belly. A horse with some dwarf traits may be perfectly healthy and make a fine pet, but others have problems with bones and teeth that make life painful for them. Dwarfs cannot be registered as miniature horses. As miniature horse breeding improves, fewer dwarfs are born.

Being a Stallion

The most valuable horses in any breed are the males, called stallions. A mare can have only one foal each year. But a stallion can mate with many mares every year and father a number of foals. An especially fine stallion can have a very important effect on a breed. For example, all Morgan horses can be traced to just one stallion, while all Thoroughbreds share just three stallions in their background.

Shadow Oaks Top Banana, AMHA National Grand Champion, owned by Ron and Sami Scheuring, is a fine example of a beautiful miniature horse.

This miniature stallion doesn't seem to know his own size as he challenges another horse.

A miniature horse stallion seems not to notice his own small size. He will challenge other males by whinnying and prancing about with his neck arched. Never mind if his rival is twice as tall. Miniature horse breeders take special care of their valuable stallions, usually keeping them in barn stalls away from the mares most of the time. That way, they can choose which stallion will breed with which mare and when.

A Gentle Breed

One important trait is very common in miniature horses, and that's gentle friendliness to humans. These horses seem to enjoy human company, even that of strangers. Maybe this is because they are so often handled, due to their small size. It's difficult to resist picking up a fluffy miniature horse foal, carrying it around, and petting it. And because of their small size, minis are easier to handle than full-sized horses.

It's easy to make friends with a mini.

3
Showing Off

Humans enjoy competition, whether for themselves or the things they own. A horse show is a fun event, where people can compare their talents and those of their horses with others. Horse shows are also important for another reason. A horse that collects blue ribbons is worth more than one that doesn't. Winning in shows is an indication that a horse meets with the standards of the breed, or that it is well trained.

Getting Ready for the Show Ring

The air smells of hay and horses and tingles with excitement. Soon the show will begin, and the families are getting their horses ready for the ring. Before any miniature horse can be shown, it must be measured to make sure it meets the height standards of the breed. Show officials use a standard measuring device, and all horses are measured at the same place with the same device. The horse must stand with its feet straight under its body. If a horse is too tall, it won't be allowed to compete.

The long hair that grows above their feet and under their chins is trimmed. Since minis have especially long, thick coats, the body

Amber Owens and Rivenburgh's Sandelee are winners.

Before it can compete, each horse is measured to make sure it is small enough to qualify in the competition.

hair is usually also cut close. Just before entering the ring, the coat is oiled to make it shine. The hooves are washed, cleaned, and buffed. Often, the hooves of dark horses are painted shiny black. The hooves of horses with white legs are usually left natural and are coated with clear hoof paint to make them shine.

Miniature Horse Shows Are Special

All horse shows feature certain events, such as selecting the best-looking horses of both sexes and different ages. But since miniature horses are easier for children to handle than big horses, the shows have many classes especially for children.

These are called youth showmanship classes. Here, what matters is not the beauty of the horse, it's how the child handles the animal. Each exhibitor in a showmanship class must wear a hat and boots and be neatly dressed. He or she is also responsible for how the horse looks. It should be in good physical condition, have its mane and tail free of tangles, and its hooves clean and properly trimmed.

The most important thing is how well the exhibitor shows off the horse. He or she should lead the animal well and be able to move the horse as the judge directs. The exhibitor also poses the horse and keeps alert to what's happening in the ring. It takes talent and practice to learn how to show off a horse well, and with minis, a child can start learning very young.

Performance in the Ring

Minis get a chance to demonstrate their training in shows. Because miniature horses can pull carts and buggies, driving classes are popular at shows. The horses are shown at a walk and a trot.

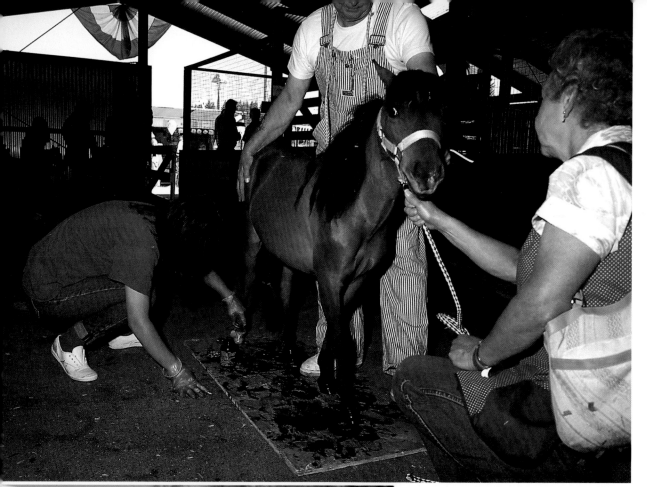

The hooves of dark-colored horses are often painted black before showing.

Chris Hunter and Little King's Wee Wish in the ring being checked over by the judge.

The handler's job is to show off the horse to its best advantage.

Miniature horses are just the right size for pulling light carts like this one.

In these classes, the most important things are the performance of the animal and how well the vehicle, horse, and driver work together and how good they look together.

Like other horses, minis can jump, and their jumping ability is tested in shows. Full-sized horses are ridden in jumping classes. But since minis are too small to ride, the handler must run alongside the horse rather than ride it.

There are two kinds of events in which horses jump over fences—

regular jumping classes and hunter classes. In regular jumping classes, handlers lead the horses through a course of at least four different jumps between 18 and 24 inches high. What matters is how high the animal can jump. If it knocks down a jump or refuses to go over, it loses points.

If horses are tied in points after the first round, the obstacles can be raised in height and the animals that have tied go over the course again. If they still tie after the obstacles are 34 inches tall, the horse that completed the course most quickly wins.

In jumping classes, the handler gets as much exercise as the horse.

In hunter classes, how the horse looks while jumping and while moving between jumps matters most. Each horse goes over the course only once.

Another performance class that is getting more and more popular is one in which the horse and handler must manage a series of obstacles. There are gates to pass through, boards to walk over, hay bales to squeeze between. The horse must be very calm and well trained and must trust its handler, or it will become frightened and refuse to cooperate.

The beauty of the jump is what matters in hunter classes.

Obstacle courses are becoming more popular in miniature horse shows.

The Most Beautiful Horses

Classes where beauty and conformation (how well the horse meets the standards of appearance for the breed) are judged are called halter classes. The halter classes in miniature horse shows are divided up by sex, age, and size of the animals. There are classes for weanlings, yearlings, and two-year-olds, and the adult horses compete separately by size. Within each sex of adult horses, those 28 inches and under are in one class, while those from 28 to 30 inches are in another. Those from 30 to 32 inches have a different

Showing young minis requires some bending and kneeling when the handler is an adult.

This handler is being playful with her horse while waiting to be judged.

class, while the biggest minis—those from 32 to 34 inches—compete separately.

Often, a miniature horse show will also feature a special class for the horse that best meets the model look of the stock-type horse and a separate class for the model refined horse. Classes for color—

Miniature horse shows often have classes for the most colorful horses.

A beautiful mini warms up before entering the show ring.

pintos and Appaloosas in one and all other colors in another—can also be offered.

Even though horses of different breeds have their own special look, certain traits are important in any breed, including miniature horses. Legs are the basis of any horse's movement, and they should be straight and set under the body, not out to the sides. The feet should point straight ahead, not toeing out or in. The horse's back should be relatively short and level.

The neck on a beautiful horse is long and nicely arched, and its head is attractive, with large, bright eyes. The bridge of the nose

should be either straight or dished, and the ears should prick up straight, not out to the sides.

Best of the Best

After the different classes in a group, such as all those for young (called "junior") mares or all those for adult stallions, are finished, the winners of each class compete against one another for the title

Time to choose the Supreme Champion.

of Group Grand Champion. For example, the winning older mares of each size class compete for Grand Champion Senior Mare. The horse placing second in each group is called the Reserve Champion.

The most exciting moment at the show is when all these winners (Grand Champion Junior and Senior Stallion, Grand Champion Junior and Senior Mare, and Grand Champion Junior and Senior

Gelding) all gather together in the ring for the judge to pick out what he or she considers the most beautiful of all the winners in the show, male and female, young and full grown. This animal is called the Supreme Halter Champion, the horse that comes closest of all entered in the show to being the ideal miniature horse.

40

4
Minis at Home

People fall in love with miniature horses for many reasons. Some mini owners once raised full-sized horses but now have retired and moved to smaller property where they can't keep big horses. By having minis, they can still share their love with horses, even though they don't have a lot of room.

Minis are just the right size for children to handle.

A mini can take its owner for a pleasant ride in the country.

Other people keep minis because they want their children to be able to learn to ride safely while very young. Adults are too heavy to ride miniatures, but young children up to 60 pounds can. Minis are also good for people with health problems that can make it impossible or dangerous for them to ride. By driving a cart hitched to one or two miniature horses, these people can have fun and travel safely around the neighborhood. A trained miniature driving horse can pull two adults for ten miles with no difficulty.

Minis are also very good as visitors for retirement homes and disabled people. Their friendly nature and their great appeal provide a fun and satisfying experience.

Minis are great for lifting the spirits of handicapped children.

Buying a Miniature Horse

Unfortunately, miniature horses are very expensive. The best show horses sell for thousands of dollars, with stallions being the most expensive. But a miniature horse breeder often has horses that are not perfect enough to be champions or to use as breeding stock. These animals may be bought for a few hundred dollars.

The least expensive and best miniature horse for family fun is a gelding. Geldings are male horses that are not perfect enough to be used for breeding. The organs that make their male hormones, the testes, are removed. Because their bodies don't produce the male hormones, geldings are calmer than stallions. And because they can't breed and are not as perfect, they are not as valuable.

A team of minis can pull a wagon full of riders.

Geldings also make especially good horses for driving because they are stronger than mares.

Taking Care of Minis

Big horses need lots of room to run. But two minis can live well on only one acre without extra feeding in the summertime. While a full-sized riding horse eats about a bale of hay every week during the winter, one bale will feed a mini for a month. So even though minis can cost a lot, they are much less expensive to keep than big horses. Feeding a mini costs less than buying food for a large dog.

Minis are easy to transport, too. Big horses need trailers pulled behind a car or truck. But minis can fit in a pickup with a camper top. And unlike big horses, miniatures don't need to wear horseshoes since they are not used very much for riding or working. As a matter of fact, minis in shows are not allowed to wear shoes.

Enjoying Minis

Some miniature horses become as much a part of the family as a dog or a cat. Now and then, people may even let their pint-sized horses into the house

But even those who can't own a miniature horse can still enjoy them. These charming animals have become so popular that now they are being raised all over the country. So if you want to see miniature horses for yourself, go to a show at the county fair or find a breeder that lives near your home. Some breeders offer shows and wagon rides for visitors during the summer. So take a family trip to visit this new and wonderful kind of horse.

Minis make good companions for children.

Index